# Sold To My Ex's Dad

Virgin Auction Romance

Kaci Rose

Five Little Roses Publishing

# Copyright

Book Cover By: **Cover Girl Design**

Editing By: Debbe @ **On The Page, Author and PA Services**

# Dedication

To Megan and Dylan who have been helping me plan the Club Red series as I slowly lose my mind with all the details.

# Blurb

He's her ex-boyfriend's dad, and she has nothing to lose. For the right bid, she can be his for the night...

**Aspen**

I'm a week away from losing everything if I can't pay my mom's medical bills and funeral expenses.

I'm so thankful she isn't around now to see what I'm about to do.

I'm about to auction off the last thing of value I have.

My V-card.

**Evan**

I'm out celebrating my friend's divorce when she walks on stage.

Aspen, my son's ex-girlfriend.

I can't take my eyes off her in barely any clothes. Then it hits me, she is auctioning off her V-card.

When the guy at the table next to me places his bid, I lose it and the next thing I know she's sitting on my bed waiting for me to make the next move.

I bought her V-card, but can I actually take it without losing the only family I have left?Step inside the world of The Auction Series, where the highest bidder wins. It's not goods and services on stage to be bought and sold, but people who have put their bodies in the spotlight. When the hammer comes down and the amount is paid, will love be the real currency?

Join some of your favorite romance authors as they take you behind the auction room doors.

# Contents

Get Free Books!                    IX

1.  Chapter 1                       1

2.  Chapter 2                       6

3.  Chapter 3                      12

4.  Chapter 4                      18

5.  Chapter 5                      25

6.  Chapter 6                      32

7.  Chapter 7                      38

8.  Chapter 8                      44

9.  Chapter 9                      50

10.  Chapter 10                    55

11.  Chapter 11                    61

12.  Chapter 12                    68

13.  Chapter 13                    74

14.  Chapter 14                    81

15. Chapter 15                        86

16. Chapter 16                        92

17. Epilogue                          98

18. Connect with Kaci Rose            106

19. Other Books by Kaci Rose          108

20.  About Kaci Rose                  111

Please Leave a Review!                112

# Get Free Books!

Do you like Military Men? Best friends brothers?
What about sweet, sexy, and addicting books?

**If you join Kaci Rose's Newsletter you get these books free!**

**https://www.kacirose.com/free-books/**
**Now on to the story!**

# Chapter 1

## Aspen

"There has to be a way that I can keep my house," I tell my best friend Willow for what feels like the hundredth time as we're looking through articles online about how to make money quickly.

Almost everything that we have come across looks like a scam with headlines like 'make $20,000 at home this week.' I'm pretty sure the ads were to trick women into sex trafficking.

Willow has a very different need to make money than I do. For her, it's all about safety and getting out of town and out from under the debt that her dad left her. For me, it's all about being able to keep my house and pay off my mom's medical bills after she died.

A few hours later, I'm about to give up hope when Willow finally strikes something.

"Okay, so somehow, I ended up on this sugar baby website. While I know neither of us wants to go the sugar daddy route, they do have some good ideas. Though their ideas are very out-of-the-box thinking. Maybe we should soak these in and sleep on them tonight and see what options sound ok in the morning. All right?," she says, looking at me.

Great, if we're down to that kind of option, I'm about to lose my house and everything that I have left.

"Okay, let's hear it."

"So, this one is more along the lines of what I need. It's a modern day mail-order bride service. Sort of like online dating, but instead of looking for a date, he's looking for a wife. The man basically pays for me to move out there with him. They list specific criteria. Just taking a quick glance, many are cowboys looking for someone to keep house and cook. I do have the option to not marry him, but it's all done within the period of a few weeks."

We look over the website that's been recommended, and it seems legit. But she's right, that's more for her. I don't want to move and give up everything because I want to stay right here.

Moving out of town, at least for now, would be best. But you gamble never knowing what kind of man you are tying yourself down to.

"That sounds great for you, but I would definitely get more information. Like how long you have to stay married before you don't have to pay the money back. Especially since the company headquarters looks to be right here in Chicago."

Willow goes back to the original webpage and starts going down a few ideas, each one less appealing than the last.

The Ideas range from selling your used underwear online to starring in a porno.

"Okay, here's one that I think you should give some serious consideration to and hear me out before you immediately reject it," Willow says, staring at me.

"Fine. I will give it serious thought. What is it?"

"Have you heard of Club Red here in Chicago?" she asks and then pulls up the Club Red website.

The website shows it's one of those BDSM sex clubs that we read about in the romance novels we like to share. I knew they existed, but I've never actually been to one or really looked one up online. Though It looks really classy and if I'm being honest a little fun.

"I know what it is. But I didn't realize there is one here in Chicago." I shrug it off waiting to see what she says next.

"Well, the club is doing a virgin auction."

"Did I just hear you right? You want me to auction off my virginity?" I ask in complete shock.

"I would totally do it if I was still a virgin, so hear me out. Your first time is going to suck anyway, so why not get paid for it? Not only will you get paid more than what you need to pay off the debt and keep the house, but it'll give you enough to go to school. You lose your V-card and only have to spend a week with the guy. Then you never have to see him again."

In shock, I stare at Willow because she is absolutely serious.

"Listen, just think about it. I'm going to go to sleep now so that I can call this mail-order bride company first thing in the morning." Willow packs up her computer and heads upstairs. She's been staying with me in the guest bedroom for the past couple of weeks.

We both need money and no matter the amount of extra shifts or even extra jobs we pick up, we won't make the type of money that we need in time. I look around the house where I grew up and the one my mom raised me as a single mother. She worked hard and spent all her money trying to give me a stable home.

The stack of bills on the dining room table seems to be mocking me. Angry red stamps all over them, telling me this is my final chance to pay. At the time, taking a second mortgage on the house in order to help my mom get better sounded like a good idea.

Her doctors were so sure she could beat this. After she was better, we would both work and pay it off while I went to night classes. We had a plan, dammit. Then one morning she was just too weak to get out of bed. Her doctors said the cancer took an aggressive turn, and it was nothing like he had seen before. She died a week later.

That was only a few months ago and the debt collectors didn't waste any time calling in anything that was in my mom's name.

The thought of losing this house is more than I can bear, and the big red foreclosure letters on the envelopes from the mail today mock me as I sit at the dining room table.

I'm out of time and I have to do something fast, but can I really sell my virginity?

# Chapter 2

## Evan

This is really the last place I want to be tonight, but my buddy wanted to go out to celebrate his divorce and being free again. Of course, there's no way I can tell him no. Not after everything he's been through with his toxic ex and her cheating and lies. He's finally free, and that is definitely something to celebrate.

So here I am at Club Red for some kind of event that he insisted is the perfect way to kick off his newfound freedom. I figure I can come and show my support, have a few drinks and slip out as everyone gets too drunk to notice that I'm no longer there. Then in the morning, I can call to check on them and no one will be the wiser.

"Come on, man, tell me you're finally going to loosen up and get laid tonight. How long has it been since you've been with a woman? It's been almost a decade since you've been in any kind of relationship," my buddy Marcus says.

He's not wrong. Being a single dad, a relationship was the last thing on my mind. My main focus was on making sure that my son was taken care of while devoting my time to him. Though, I'm not going to admit to the last time that I've been with a woman.

They don't need to know that it's been years since I've been with anyone. Not since my son brought home, Aspen. They were dating at the time, and she captivated me in a way I can't even describe. They have since broken up and to this day we've been nothing more than friends, but I can't even look at another woman without thinking about her.

She may be nineteen, but she's still way too young for me. Though that hasn't stopped me from watching her and thinking about her. Chances are no woman will match up to her and until I can move past her, there will be no one else.

When she was dating my son, at least they would come over for dinner and I'd get my fix from talking to her. While she was there with my son, I would cook dinner with her and spend time with her. Even that little bit of time was enough.

We would throw a movie and game night. My son and she would have friends over to use the pool. To this very day, Aspen, in a bikini still haunts my dreams.

Since they've broken up, it's been more difficult to see her. I have even ventured into what many might call stalking territory. With the need to take care of her, I frequently leave groceries on her doorstep making sure that she eats.

But I don't just leave healthy food either. I make sure all her favorites are there. I even went as far as buying that crappy diner where she works so I could give her a raise so she can pay her bills. Any time she asks for more shifts she gets them, even if no one is really needed.

When her mom died, I made sure to show up at the funeral and support her. Against her will, I also took care of some of the funeral costs. At that point, she was so happy to have a familiar face that she leaned on me the whole day and let me take control. Not only did I hate every tear that fell from her eyes, I hated how sad she was. But being able to take care of her in that manner? It was still one of the best days. No reason needed to have her in my arms. She was there and made no point in trying to leave.

On that day, I didn't leave her side. When people started to hang on too long, I would move them along, making sure she ate and had something to drink. Even going so far as to make sure she was where she needed to be. I let her wallow in her grief, and she trusted me to make sure that everything was taken care of properly.

Had she been mine, that night after everyone left, I would have taken her upstairs and made love to her until she forgot that she had a reason to be sad and upset. But she wasn't mine and no matter how much I wanted to it just wouldn't have been right. Aspen is always going to be my son's ex-girlfriend, and my son is the only family I have left.

As I'm thinking about Aspen, whatever event we're at starts and I don't pay too much attention. Women that are barely dressed come out on stage and the men are bidding. I'm guessing to spend some time with these women for the night. Most of them look barely eighteen and not one of them catches my attention or even causes my dick to stiffen.

I order another drink, figuring that after this auction the guys will be thoroughly entertained, and I could sneak out. I'm not really keeping track of many of the women on the stage. Though a few of the guys have placed some bids and are having a good time. But by the time I get my drink, I happen to glance up and the woman walking out on stage catches my attention.

Aspen.

What's the fuck is this girl doing on stage wearing practically nothing? It's bad enough she's showing off all of her curves, but the clothes she's wearing are so thin I can see the outline and the color of her nipples.

"What was this event again?" I ask Marcus, who's sitting beside me.

He laughs, "Finally, see something you like? It's a virgin auction where you're buying the girl's virginity. Have at it. It'll be great to see you let loose for once."

Why the hell is Aspen selling her virginity? Is she in some kind of trouble and I didn't know? What has she gotten herself into? Why didn't she come to me?

Bidding starts and the guy next to me places a bid. I glare him down as I stand up. I'm not a violent person, but I've never wanted to punch someone in the face as much as I do right now.

What the fuck is going on?

# Chapter 3

## Aspen

I have never been so scared in my entire life. Not when my mom was sick and not when she died. But standing up here getting ready to go out on stage, I think I'm about to throw up.

After I signed up for the auction at Club Red, they called me in and went over everything. They had me sign so many papers stating the guys were buying time with a virgin, not my virginity specifically. Some sort of legal thing, I guess.

Once I signed the papers, I was whisked away to have every inch of me buffed, polished, waxed, and trimmed. When I looked in the mirror after they did my hair and makeup tonight, I swear I didn't look like myself. Then they got me dressed.

What I'm wearing looks more like something you wear in the bedroom. It's pretty much see through and covers nothing.

"You're up, Aspen." The woman on the side of the stage who has been running things calls.

She puts a hand on my back and gives me a little push out on stage. I don't even make it to the spot I was told to stand on before bidding starts. My face has to be as red as their logo and I think there is no way I'm going to make enough money. One look at me and you know I have no idea what I'm doing.

The lady in charge, whose name I still don't know, says the men will eat that up. If they wanted experience, they wouldn't be spending money on a virgin.

I make it to the spot on the stage, and I finally hear the next bid. Are they really up to bidding $500,000 already? The last girl only got $160,000!

Another bid goes up, and then a man in the back stands up. I can't see anything but a shadow of the man's figure.

"Five million dollars!" he calls out, and the room goes quiet.

My jaw drops. This man just bid five million dollars for my virginity. I only needed about one hundred grand. Anything over would allow me to go to school, but five million. Holy shit.

The man walks to the stage, and that's when I see it's Mr. Warner, my ex-boyfriend Brett's dad! Not only that, but he looks pissed.

No one says another word as he walks to the stage and the auctioneer regains his composure.

"Going once, going twice, and sold to the gentleman walking toward the stage." People in the room start whispering, including the girls behind me still waiting to go up on stage.

The moment Mr. Warner reaches the stage, he shrugs out of his jacket and hands it to me.

"Put this on, Aspen." He says in a flat tone.

As he instructed, I take his jacket and put it on, following him over to the area where he will make his payment. His jacket is warm and soft. The inside is silk and feels like butter.

Mr. Warner has spent his life building his company and is a billionaire. To him, this five million will be a drop in the bucket. But to me it means everything. Hell, his suit jacket alone probably cost more than I make in an entire year.

Once he pays, we are led to an elevator and up to the second floor to a private room. For the first time that night, we are left alone. I walk over to the couch against the wall and sit down, hoping he won't see how badly I'm shaking.

When I finally look at him, he is staring me down. His eyes are running over my body and when I glance down, it's impossible to miss how hard he is. Tonight I thought I'd lose my virginity to some unknown old man, spend a few days with him, and be on my way.

This complicates things immensely. Not to mention I have a huge crush on this man, always have. He's an older version of Brett, more mature, nicer and sexier all the way around.

"Why did you do this?" He asks when he finally speaks.

The big question I knew was coming. I look down at my lap. It was never my attention to admit how difficult things were to Mr. Warner. Under no circumstances did I ever want him to think I was angling for a handout.

"Mr. Warner I..."

He cuts me off with a bitter laugh.

"I just paid five million dollars to stick my dick in my son's ex-girlfriend. The least you can do is call me Evan."

I cringe, then clear my throat and try again.

"Evan, I'm sorry about tonight. I just didn't have another choice."

"You could have come to me, told me what was going on, and I'd have been happy to help."

"But I'm not dating Brett anymore."

"That doesn't matter. I like to think we became friends while you were with my son. Didn't we?"

I nod.

"Then at your mom's funeral..."

I nod again.

He walks up to me and kneels down in front of me. His hand tilts my chin until I'm looking into his eyes.

"Tell me." He whispers, his eyes searching mine.

"When my mom got sick, she lost her job and her insurance. The medical bills piled up and her doctor was sure she'd recovered because she was doing so well. So, we used my college fund and took a second mortgage on the house to pay for her treatment and we had a plan to pay it off. The plan was for me to go to school later. Then she took a turn for the worse and within a week was gone. I have a stack of medical bills and I am about to lose my house. You should have seen my mom the day we moved in there. She worked so hard as a single mom to buy that place. I just couldn't bear to lose it."

He wipes a tear away with his thumb as I take a few deep breaths to steady myself.

"You could have come to me, baby girl, though I will say I think I like this option much better."

# Chapter 4

## Evan

She looks so damn beautiful sitting here in my jacket in the dim light. Her makeup is all done up, and she doesn't quite look like the girl that I've fallen for. With all the makeup on, she looks older, and maybe that's why my guard is down more than it should be.

My brain is saying give her the money and walk away. But my heart and body want her more than I ever thought possible, and they aren't letting me get up and walk away.

"Why didn't you come to me?" I whisper without thinking. My mind is racing with the things I could have done differently. If I'd only let her know, she could have come to me for money, instead of resorting to this drastic measure. Maybe I shouldn't have kept my distance after she and my son broke up, and especially not after her mom's funeral.

"Outside of my mom's funeral, we haven't seen each other in a year. It didn't occur to me to ask my ex's dad."

Of course, she didn't think about it because she didn't know my feelings for her. All because I thought that keeping my distance was the right thing to do. Maybe if I hadn't, she would have felt she could come talk to me and she wouldn't have had to resort to this.

I thought keeping my feelings to myself was the right thing to do because I didn't want to do anything to jeopardize my relationship with my son regardless of what my feelings were Aspen are.

But if it means stopping her from making decisions like this and having to do something so outside of her character to take care of herself, then the risk with Brett is just something I'm going to have to take.

When that other asshole was bidding on her earlier, I wanted to kill him, and I'm not usually someone who is so violent. Yet the thought of any other man putting their hands on her was just more than I could take.

"Should I get on the bed now?" she asks in such an innocent voice.

"Fuck"

Standing up, I take a few steps away from her, because just that question alone and the thought of her on the bed has my dick hard as nails. I want her. There's no question about it and after just spending five million, there's nothing in the way to stop me from having her. But not here and not like this.

"I have an entire week with you. I'm not going to fuck you here, baby girl. Get dressed. We're going to go back to my place."

"Okay." She stands, taking a deep breath, and moves towards the door.

"But make no mistake. Your virginity is mine." Though I didn't plan on saying it, much less saying it in my deep commanding voice, but now it's out there. A sexy as hell pink stain coats her cheeks, and she nods her head before going out the door. As I'm following her, she turns right down the hallway instead of left towards the front door.

"Where are you going?" She stops and turns around.

"My things are in a locker in the back room. I'll be right back." She continues walking down the hall.

"I'm not letting you out of my sight. At least, not here. I will come with you."

"Oh, I don't think you'll be allowed in the back."

"You let me worry about that." I wrap a protective arm around her waist and follow her back down the hallway and downstairs to the locker room.

Leaving on the barely there number she wore on stage, she slips her jeans and a T-shirt on over it. Although she tries to hand me my jacket, I place it back over her since I know it's going to be colder outside, and she doesn't seem to have a coat with her.

In my car on the way back to my place, she's nervous. Constantly, she's fidgeting and every so often looks over at me before looking back out the window. Before tonight, things were so easy with us and she was always relaxed around me, and I want that back. But I know right now it's not going to happen.

I make a mental note that I need to call the office and tell them that I'm not going to be in this week. There's absolutely no way I'm going to miss any time with her. Not even one minute, if I can help it. Being as I own the company, taking time off isn't going to be an issue. But I will shock some people because I haven't taken time off of work for more than a day in many years.

Once we're at my home, she hesitantly walks through the door. Since she and Brett broke up, it's been about a year that she's been here. Not much has changed other than I got a new TV, a bigger one.

"Will he be here?"

I don't bother playing stupid trying to figure out who she means. I know she means Brett. Since I don't want him to know about this either, I'm not surprised that she's concerned. But there is something that I need to know.

"No, he won't be here at all this week." I watch her visibly relax, which makes me want to know the answer to the next question even more.

"Why did you guys break up?"

"What did he say?"

"That it wasn't working out."

She gives a bit of a dry laugh and shakes her head, not meeting my eyes.

"The short version is my mom got sick and I wouldn't put out, so he dumped me for a girl who did."

I'm down on the other end of the couch from her, giving her some space, but not too much.

"He's an idiot." Even though I mean that more than she realizes, in the back of my head, I'm secretly thrilled that they never had sex. I had always assumed they did.

"Is the money from tonight going to be enough?" I asked needing to make sure that she's taken care of, and everything will be paid off. I don't need her pulling a stunt like this again. Though by the time I'm done with her, she won't qualify for another virgin auction.

"It's way more than enough. The money will pay off the bills and the house. Plus, I could go to school ten times over to Harvard and still have money left over."

Like a magnet being drawn to her, I scoot closer, and she doesn't move back. To my surprise, she moves towards me just a bit.

"Good," I say.

When she smiles up at me, a piece of hair falls into her face and without thinking, I reach up and tuck it back behind her ear.

Her dark brown eyes meet mine, and that connection that I always felt between us is there. It makes me wonder if she feels it too. It's the kind of contact that pulls me in and makes me want to kiss her. Though every time I felt it before now, I've always stopped myself. But

I'm not stopping this time. She's mine for the week. Slowly I lean in, giving her plenty of time to stop me, but she doesn't. Instead, she wraps a hand behind my neck and pulls me in.

The moment her lips touch mine, I know I will never come back from this week. Letting her go will rip my heart out, but if I have to, I will let her go. The memories of this week will have to be what I cling to.

More times than I want to admit, I imagined a kiss like this. Her lips on mine, and her hands on me. I want more. Wrapping my hand in her hair, I pull her closer and she comes to me easily.

She may only be kissing my lips, but I feel it all over my body and my dick wonders what it would be like to have these soft lips around it.

Fuck, one week will never be enough.

# Chapter 5

## Aspen

Holy Shit. Mr. Warner... Evan. Evan is kissing me.

And he's really good at it. Like really, really good.

Hell, it's such a turn on with his hand in my hair and his lips on mine. Every time his tongue stokes mine, I swear I get even wetter. I want him so damn much and I didn't care if he had taken me in the room at Club Red. Even then, I was more than ready.

Not wanting him to stop, I wrap my arms around his neck and run one of my hands through his hair like I have had to stop myself from doing many times.

With my hands on him, he lets out a small moan that I feel all the way to my core.

"Mr. Warner," I say the first chance I'm able to take a breath.

"Call me Evan, baby girl," he whispers back. Then his lips are on mine again, completely erasing my mind of whatever I was going to say. When he pulls back, I try again.

"Evan," is all I get out.

His whole body shudders when I say his name. Then, with his eyes closed, he rests his forehead on mine. All I can do is sit there soaking him in and enjoy being so close and touching me.

He wraps his hands around my waist and the next thing I know, I'm sitting on his lap, right there on the couch in the middle of his living room. A living room that I had spent many times with Brett and him, watching TV, and even playing board games.

Instinctively, I wrap my arms around his neck, and he smiles like that was exactly what he wanted me to do. He kisses my temple before pulling away just enough to look me in the eye.

"Here's how this is going to go. I get one week with you. In that time, your virginity is mine, but I'm not going to force you, and I don't want you scared."

My eyes go wide. What in the world gave him the impression that I would be scared of him?

I've done a better job than I thought hiding how I felt about him. But I've always had a crush on him and the last thing I would be is scared, especially not of him.

"The first day you walked in on Brett's arm, I wanted you then. I shouldn't have. You were only weeks away from your eighteenth birthday. When you dated Brett, you guys were over here all the time, and I enjoyed spending time with you. At the time, that was enough."

"But when we broke up..." he squeezes my hip to stop me from talking.

"When you two broke up, I still wanted you. But because Brett is my son, it didn't change things. I kept telling myself how wrong it was, but I never stopped watching after you. Had I known you were in this kind of trouble, I would have taken care of it and never would it have gotten this far. But there's no question, I will have you."

Now it's my body's turn to let out an involuntary shimmer as he starts rubbing his hands up and down my back. But all it does is get it impossible for me to think about anything else other than where else I wish he would put his hands.

"I've always had such a crush on you, too. It was me who was always insisting we hang out here instead of going out and doing things because I wanted to be near you. I never could admit that to Brett. Even though I think in reality, I knew it was over with him long before he dumped me, I just didn't want to lose you."

He nods and stares at the wall across from the couch for a moment like he's trying to make a big decision.

"Well, it's good that now it's all out in the open, and we know where each other stand. Why don't you get ready for bed? You'll be sleeping in my bed with me."

Right now I'm thankful that the club told me to pack a bag of things that I would need, but just the essentials. So I at least have a toothbrush here. But I want to push my luck with one more thing.

"Is it possible to check my email before we go to bed?"

"Why do you need to check your email? Is everything okay? His face fills with concern.

"I want to see if my friend Willow has checked in. She too needed money and decided to go for a mail-order bride option. They matched her with a guy out in Montana and she promised to email and check in, letting me know how it was going. Especially since neither of us would have a contact phone number for a while."

He cusses under his breath and shakes his head before gently lifting me to stand up. Without a word, he takes my hand, leading me towards his office and sits me down and starts up his work computer. When he pulls up the browser and turns to me, I freeze.

"What's wrong?" he asks

"This is your work computer," I say, as if that should explain everything and in my mind, it should.

"Yes. You said you need to check your email."

"But no one touches your work computer. You don't even let Brett touch it," I say, remembering the time that Brett's computer was in the shop, and he asked his dad to use the computer for a school project. But his dad wouldn't let him, and instead made him use the laptop saying no one is to ever touch his work computer. Yet here he is freely offering it to me.

"If I did not trust you to use it, I would not have offered it to you."

He gives me a pointed look, making his meaning clear. He trusts me to use it, but he didn't trust Brett. I nod, bring up my email to check for anything from Willow.

Pulling his phone out, he makes a phone call and steps out into the hallway.

Scanning my email, which is mostly junk. I don't see anything from her. So I send her a short message telling her that I'm safe, who bought me, and a quick overview of what happened at the auction. Finally, I tell her I'll check my email again in a few days.

Though I try not to eavesdrop on Evan's conversation in the hall, it's hard not to hear what he's saying. Apparently, he's on with someone in the office and whoever picked up the phone is shocked that he's taking the time off. He's convincing them that he's not sick or dying, but simply decided to take a week off, and he'll be checking his email in case he's needed.

As I close out my email, he wraps up his phone call and walks back into the room.

"Anything from your friend?"

"Nope. Not yet, but I sent her a message letting her know that I was safe and okay."

"Well, if you don't hear from her soon, you let me know and I'll get one of my guys to figure out where she's at and make sure that she's all right."

I stand up from the desk a little awkwardly, not sure what to do next.

"Are you ready for bed now, baby girl?"

# Chapter 6

## Evan

To say the staff in my office is shocked would be an understatement. I will easily admit I'm a workaholic. It's gotten me where I am today, a billionaire. While I don't spend frivolously, I don't want for anything either.

Well, I don't want for anything except for Aspen and spending five million on her is the most frivolous thing I've ever spent my money on.

Of course, as soon as they hear I'm not going to be in for a week, a million questions start flying. I tell them to deal with it, and if they can't figure it out, email me. What I don't tell them is I have absolutely no intention of checking my email or address any business concerns. My sole focus is going to be on Aspen for the entire week. For all I care, my company could crash and burn.

I only get one week with Aspen and I'm not giving up a single minute of it because these memories from this week will have to last me until I'm on my deathbed.

Right now, Aspen is in the bathroom getting ready for bed. While I know that I should give her a space in the guest room, I'm just enough of a bastard to keep her close. I want to be able to wrap my arms around her and know what it's like to have her sleeping next to me and not wake up alone for the first time in years.

No, I try not to think about what she's doing in the bathroom to get ready for bed. Otherwise, I might not be able to give her the privacy she deserves. Then a thought hits me as she's getting ready for bed.

"Do you need to take care of any of the loans so that you can enjoy your week here?" I ask through the door of the bathroom.

"Yes, but all the paperwork is back at my house."

"Tomorrow, we'll head over there and you can get what you need and pack a bag of anything you want to bring with you for the week, clothes or whatever."

Plus, it'll give me a chance to check out the house and see how she's been really doing, not just what she's willing to let me know. I tell myself it's so I can get an idea of how I can help her out, not just so that I can see how she lives in her space and know what it's like to be in her space. There's some shuffling on the other side of the door and all I can think about is her getting ready for bed in that outfit that she wore on stage earlier.

"You still have that outfit you wore onstage?"

"Yes."

"Wear it to bed tonight."

She doesn't say anything, but all the noise on the other side of the door stops for just a moment before I hear her getting ready for bed again. I smile to myself, stepping into the closet and changing out of my suit.

For a second, I hesitate on what to wear to bed, but decide on just my boxers. Then I make my way to the bed, climb in, sitting with my back to the headboard and watching the bathroom door waiting for her to come out.

When she steps out in that black barely there lace outfit, my dick goes hard instantly. Hesitantly, she stands by the door looking shy and cute as hell, before quickly scurrying to the other side of the bed. Then hurriedly pulls the covers up hiding her body from me.

Reaching over, I rip the covers away and her eyes go wide.

"You are so damn beautiful," I say. Almost like my hand has a mind of its own, it reaches up and runs along the side of her throat, tracing along the pulse point before slowly moving down to lightly trace over the top of her breasts.

"Don't hide your body from me." I run a finger over her already hard nipples, and she just nods at me in agreement.

Her breathing picks up as I slowly trace down the center of her stomach and stop just at the top of the tiny strip of fabric that separates me from what I paid five million for.

I should stop. I should cover her back up and let her go to sleep. But I have to know, so I lightly move a finger down her panty-covered slit and when I find the material soaking wet, I know there's no way we're just going to bed.

"Do you need to come, baby girl?" At my words, her face turns bright red. Which I still haven't told her that I find it sexy as hell. When she nods, all thoughts of what I should do vanish because I can't leave her in need.

I lay on my side, propped up on my elbow so I can watch her as I slide my hand into her panties. A slight brush on her clit causes her to gasp slightly.

Running my fingers down her slit, I gather some of the wetness there and bring it to her clit. But I never take my eyes off her face, as she closes her eyes and almost purrs. Taking my time, I play with her clit and watch her reactions, learning what she likes. It's my goal to learn every bit of how to make her cum harder than she has in her whole life.

I want her to remember that I am the one who can give her such pleasure that no one else will be able to replicate. So, when I can tell she is close to cumming, I stop and slide back down to her opening. When her eyes pop open, I smile as I slide a finger into her.

Even with how wet she is, it's a tight fit, and it hits me again. She's a virgin.

Fuck.

I gently work my finger in, knowing I need to stretch her before I have her, and that won't be tonight.

When I try to add a second finger, she tenses up. I can't have that, so I lean in and kiss her. At the same time, reaching to play with her clit using my thumb. At my touch, she melts right back into the bed.

As I add a second finger, I don't stop playing with her clit and before I know it, she is clamping down around my fingers and gasping for breath. Freezing, I pull back to make sure she is okay.

She looks slightly dazed, with her eyes unfocused and her lips parted and plump from my kissing her. Slowly, I thrust in and out of her, and then her climax is right there on the edge.

"Eyes on me," I whisper. Because I want her thinking of me, knowing it's me who gives her this pleasure.

Her eyes lock on mine as I add more pressure to her clit and a moment later her body tenses up and she reaches out to grip my arm. To stop me or prevent me from stopping, I'm not sure. But the moans she lets out as her body tenses are some of the sweetest I have ever heard and know they will haunt my dreams.

As she relaxes, I remove my hand from her panties, leaning down to give her a soft kiss before putting her body against mine and pulling the covers over us.

She's far too young for me, but there is no chance in hell I'm going back now.

# Chapter 7

## Aspen

What a hell of a dream! Wait until I tell Willow. Before I even open my eyes, those are my first thoughts waking up. When I stretch my body, I realize the sheets are so much more comfortable than anything that I can afford. That's when I finally opened my eyes and realized it was not a dream. I am in Mr. Warner's bed, rather, Evan's bed.

The entire night comes flooding back to me and I bury my face in my hands. I can't believe that I actually went through with the auction. Much less that it was Brett's father that bought me for 5 million, no less.

The smell of coffee and bacon fills the air, which means Evan must be downstairs cooking breakfast. Getting up, I find his button-down shirt from last night draped over the chair, put it on, and use the bathroom before going downstairs.

I step into the doorway, and he turns to look at me. He's in sweatpants with no shirt, and my eyes rum over his very sculpted abs and his hard body, that looks nowhere near its age. Then my eyes meet his and the heat in them as they roam over my body gives me shivers and makes my body all tingly. It's the look that I remember from last night when he took such care of my body. I can feel my cheeks flush and that causes a small smile to tug at his lips.

He holds a hand out to me, and I go willingly and easily like it's the most normal thing in the world for him to be shirtless cooking breakfast and me waking up in his bed. When I reach him, he wraps an arm around my waist and kisses the top of my head before turning back to make sure he doesn't burn bacon.

"Good morning, baby girl. There's coffee over there on the counter." He nods toward the counter to my left.

I make myself a cup of coffee and he watches my every move. It's no secret to him that coffee is what keeps me going and I'm thankful he has some ready and waiting for me.

Taking my cup, I head over to the table and barely sit down before he's setting a plate of food in front of me and sitting down in the chair next to mine with his plate in front of him. He watches me take a few bites of the eggs, bacon and toast before giving me an approving nod and taking a few bites for himself.

"Do you have any questions for me? Anything you want to know?" he asks.

There are a million things which run through my mind as I finish chewing a mouthful of eggs.

"Yes, but they aren't relevant to this," I say, deciding to take the easy way out. Then I drop my eyes back down to my plate and take another bite of breakfast.

"Come on. Let's hear it," he says. "We're going to do this, so there has to be a certain element of trust between us and that will go both ways."

A small smile crosses his face, so I decide to go forward and ask my question. The worst he can say is that he doesn't want to talk about it like Brett would say when I would ask.

"I want to know about Brett's mom. He never really talked about her, so I always wondered," I ask. The smile on Evan's face falters. Then he gets a serious look and nods for a moment lost in thought.

"Well, I was young and stupid. I was fifteen, she was seventeen, and I thought I was in love. But really, she just saw my family's money and loved it when I would spend money on her. When I wouldn't spend money on what she wanted, she would make it known how upset she was. At fifteen, I didn't know any better and kept spending money on her so I would keep getting laid." He takes a sip of his coffee and almost looks mad, though I can't tell if it's mad about the subject or mad at himself or mad that he has to now open up about all this to me.

"Right before my sixteenth birthday, she found out she was pregnant. Thankfully, that's also when my parents got involved, demanded a DNA test, and got our lawyers involved. See, my parents knew that she was after our money and it's why they gave me a spending limit. I wasn't given free access to our money."

That was news to me. I had no idea that he came from family money. I had always thought that he was self-made because I know that he built his business from the ground up.

"Long story short, my dad had a great good lawyer, and we got custody of the child. Though she didn't fight too hard because she thought that she'd be riding the gravy train of child support. Well, my lawyer was smarter than that and thankfully, so were my parents and I got full custody of Brett. She got him every other weekend and to keep her happy, neither of us paid child support. When Brett was three, she stopped taking him for her weekends, claiming it was too hard while she was in college." At this point he gives a bitter laugh and glances over at me.

I reached out to take his hand to offer some comfort, but I desperately want him to continue the story.

"Once I graduated high school and started college, I used the allowance that my parents give me to hire a nanny to help with Brett while I went to school. I moved out to my parent's guest cottage, and they didn't charge me rent even though they probably should have. While I built my company, I kept the nanny on. Later, when my parents died, I merged my dad's company into mine and set it up so that I could be home as much as possible with Brett. I didn't want him raised solely by nannies. I did my best to be at every event and I can count the ones I had to miss on my hand."

I know he was a good father. Even Brett would say that they may have had their disagreements and may not have agreed on things, but Brett knew how lucky he was. He never took that for granted, but it doesn't seem like the right time to mention that.

"During that time, his mother saw him when it was convenient. Maybe a few times a year. Though she did remember to send a birthday card and a Christmas present. It seemed like all the time she tried to get money from me, but the only instances that I would give her money was for her to take Brett out to do something. Mainly because I wasn't going to deny him time with his mother simply because she couldn't afford it. His mom died when he was fourteen. A drunk driver hit her, but she had been drinking as well. The authorities determined that both of the drivers had tried to swerve to miss each other and that's what caused them to crash into each other. Brett doesn't know that his mom was also drunk and partly at fault for that accident, so I'd appreciate it if you would keep that to yourself. I'd rather him think good things about his mother."

"Of course, I completely understand. Has there been anyone else since her?"

"No one serious enough for Brett to meet, and not a single person since I met you."

# Chapter 8

## Evan

Last night I barely slept at all. I just kept thinking about how right it felt to have her in my bed and in my arms. It became crystal clear that this was about so much more than just sex for me, and it was never going to be about just sex. And then somewhere in the early hours, I made the decision that I was going to keep her.

Yes, my decision to stay with her is going to cause problems with Brett. But I know he wants me to be happy. He's told me so many times and he's asked how come he never sees me date. While this isn't exactly what he meant, he will come around. He never did really deserve her, nor did he treat her right. In hopes that she'll want to stay with me at the end of the week and never want to leave, I plan to show her how she should be treated. Little things like noticing her make her coffee, so tomorrow I'll know exactly how she likes it.

Watching her, I can see she's still a bit flustered with my confession. That's all right. It might take her some time to understand that I'm not going to hold things back. If I'm going to demand honesty from her, the least I can do is offer it in return.

"Eat up, baby girl, so we can go get your stuff resolved." That seems to kick her back into gear and she begins eating again. The moment she's done, she flies upstairs to go get ready. It almost as if she can't get away from me fast enough. I clean up the kitchen and follow her with a smile on my face. Knowing that she's going to be in my bedroom when I go up, I love seeing her there.

When we get to her house, she opens the door and lets me in, but she still seems a little unsure of herself.

"Go pack a bag of whatever you'll need for the next week," I tell her and she scurries off upstairs while I get a good look around her house. The funeral is the only other time I was ever here, and at that point I was more focused on taking care of her than actually looking around. Plus, the place was full of people.

Knowing her story and that her mom bought this place as a single mother, I can appreciate it. By far, it's nicer than the pool house Brett and I were living in when I went to school, and it's even bigger than the first place that we had together after I graduated. It feels like a home with photos everywhere and has been nicely decorated. On the wall by the door are a bunch of photos of Aspen and her mom. One is Aspen in her cap and gown at her high school graduation. I remember that day as I was there for Brett's graduation. They were still dating at the time, and I was so damn proud of her. She was glowing from ear to ear, and her mom just continued to gush about how proud she was of her.

That night, Brett and Aspen went to a friend's graduation party, and I was so sure that they were having sex. Especially since they went to prom together. I've got to say I've never been so happy to be so wrong.

When she comes down the stairs with her suitcase in her hand, I rush to take it from her. Then she walks into the kitchen area and picks up a thick binder off the dining room table.

"What's that?" I ask nodding towards the binder.

"It's all my mom's medical bills that have to be paid."

Fuck.

No wonder she was so desperate to earn money.

"Will you let me handle that? I want you to just relax this week. I know how much stress you have been under. Please let me do this for you."

She hugs the binder to her chest tightly and shakes her head.

"Oh no. You have already done so much. I can't ever thank you enough."

But when I think of her mouth around my cock, well, that would be plenty of thanks. But for now, I keep that to myself. Instead, I go for a different truth.

"I like taking care of you. Please let me." Making sure to keep my voice soft as I watch her struggle with an internal battle.

"You'll use the money from last night, right?" she asks.

"Yes."

I hate to lie to her but she wouldn't agree with any other way to use the money. But what I gave her last night is for her to do whatever she wants to do. However, I will pay off these bills and take care of her, but that would be without touching a single cent of that money. By the time she realizes what I did, there will be no way to change it.

She finally nods and hands over the binder. Watching, I can visibly see a weight lift off her shoulders. She smiles at me and seems so much more like the carefree girl I met the first time Brett brought her home.

When we get home, I send her out to go swimming and take the binder to my office and crack it open. The front is filled with the foreclosure notices on her house, so that's the first thing I handle. In less than an hour, I have her house paid off and even have her utilities paid at least for a year in advance.

Most of the medical bills are through the hospital, so I called them next and get them squared away. After paying off her car, I join her at the pool. Tomorrow, I'll tackle and pay the miscellaneous medical bills, but for now, the majority of it is taken care of and her house is safe.

Going upstairs, I slip into my swim trunks, taking a look at her through my bedroom window before heading down. How many times did I watch her and Brett from my room wishing that it was me out there with her? This time it will be me and I am planning to enjoy every minute of it.

# Chapter 9

## Aspen

It's been so long since someone has taken care of me. Before my mom got sick, she was the only one who cared, and then the roles flipped, and I took care of her. But it's nice to let go, not worry and stress over the bills.

After this week, I can't imagine what my life will be like when I don't have to pick up every possible shift I can. Hell, I can go into that crappy diner, quit and go to school full time, and not have to work while I do so.

The thought of going back to school excites me. It's fun to figure out what I want to do or what profession I want to pursue and pick out the classes I want to take. Once I get home, I can start looking and applying to the school of my choice.

Hell, there is enough money for me to travel a bit before I go to school. Maybe I will, depending on when the next round of classes starts. If not, I will travel over winter break because it's not like I have a family to spend it with. No sad thoughts today, I tell myself, and keep focusing on the good.

When I step into the pool, it's perfectly warmed and feels like heaven against my sore muscles. I guess I've been tenser than I thought. Swimming a few laps, I enjoy the water against my skin, but after a while I get out and lay on the lounger.

I put on sunscreen because I know Evan will lecture me if I don't and then I grab my phone, put on an audiobook and my earbuds as I lay down on the lounger and close my eyes. When was the last time I had nothing to do like this? I can't even remember the last time I had time to read a book.

The sun on my skin feels amazing as I get lost in the audiobook. I lose track of everything else around me. That is, until the feel of warm lips at the top of my bikini bottoms jolt me from the story.

My eyes fly open to find Evan kneeling beside my chair and looking up at me. His lips ghost up my stomach before he reaches up and kisses me on my lips ever so softly. After removing my headphones, he brushes a finger down my cheek, never taking his eyes off of me.

"Are you wearing sunscreen?"

Since I already knew he was going to ask me, I just nod slightly smiling. Then an approving look crosses his face along with a small smile. Without saying anything, he traces his fingers down my arm ever so lightly until he reaches my breasts.

Taking his time, he slips his hand into my top and starts to play with my breasts, holding them in his hands and teasing me before pulling the triangles back to expose them. I gasp and quickly look around to make sure no one else can see us.

"No one can see you. I don't like to share." He murmurs, reading my mind.

His thumbs brush over my nipples, pulling my attention back to him. Then he leans down and pulls one of my nipples into his mouth. The hot dry sun on my skin and his wet mouth on my breast give an amazing contrast in sensations.

He moves to my other nipple, giving it the same attention before kissing lightly down my stomach. When I try to cover my breasts again, he stops me.

"Don't hide these. They are too damn pretty to be covered up under that fabric." He situates himself on the end of my chair and runs his hands up my legs, spreading them wide.

I already know when he gets to my core I'm going to be soaked and not because of the swim I took earlier. It's because his lips were on me, and so are his hands, and they both drive me crazy. Just the slightest touch from him, and I'm wet and ready for anything he has to offer.

His hands grip my hips and his thumbs brush over my core before he pulls the strings holding the bikini bottoms together. As he slowly unties them, his eyes are on me like he's waiting for me to stop him, but I have no plans to obstruct him.

When his thumb brushes my clit, it feels so damn good that if he were to stop now, I think I'd go insane. Throwing my head back, I close my eyes, getting lost in the feeling of him touching me. Even though I expect to feel his hands on me again, when his tongue makes contact with my clit I jump, l Iook down at him, only to find him looking up at me.

Since I'm not stopping him, he put his mouth back on me and plays me like he's been doing it for years and not twelve hours. His mouth stays on my clit as he thrusts a finger into me.

When all I want is a relief, it's as if he wants to drag this out with his slow pace. But he is tasting me like he's doing it for his pleasure and not mine, and for some reason that is even more of a turn-on.

He's dancing around what I really need. Finally, I reach down and grab hold of his hair, holding him where I need him. I swear I can feel him smile against my skin and that's when he hooks his fingers and hits the spot he's been playing around. My body locks up and I cum even harder than I did last night, and I didn't think that was possible.

When I relax and open my eyes again, he's sitting on the edge of the lounger with a smile on his face watching me, and the tent in his pants is obvious. I lock on his eyes and without thinking I reach for him, and he stops me.

"This was about you, baby girl." He holds my hand and brings it to his mouth, placing a soft kiss in the center of my palm.

"But that was last night, and I really want to see you fall apart too. Please?" I ask.

# Chapter 10

## Evan

I can't believe this girl is asking to suck my cock. How many times have I pictured this moment? I'd be completely happy to simply take care of her, but if she is ready to take this next step, who am I to say no?

"Go get in the pool, baby girl," I tell her. Disappointment is evident on her face, but she still does as I ask.

As she gets up from the chair and fixes her swimsuit, I have to adjust my dick because it gets harder seeing all that exposed skin. Knowing I just had my hands and mouth on her, and soon will be having my cock inside of her, gets my adrenaline pumping.

I watch her body disappear beneath the water before standing up and making my way to the edge of the pool. Taking a deep breath and adjusting myself, I sit down at the edge of the pool and stick my feet in the water.

"From watching you over the years, I have many fantasies and I plan to act out as many as we can, starting here in the pool."

Her face lights up with understanding before she turns and swims to the other side of the pool. She looks back and her eyes lock with mine.

"That swimsuit you have on today is a tease. You know that. You give guys ideas they shouldn't have." I say in my fatherly voice.

"Well, I only wore it for my boyfriend, not out in front of a bunch of people." She shrugs, brushing some water from her face.

"Yet he isn't here, is he?" Though my gut twists, even pretending she belongs to someone else. But how many times did I want to do exactly what we are doing right now?

More times than I can count.

She shakes her head but remains on the other side of the pool.

"Well, it was you who made my cock hard, so why don't you get over here and suck it off before he gets back?" I smirk.

Her eyes go wide, and she takes a hesitant step toward me before gasping.

SOLD TO MY EX'S DAD

"Mr. Warner!" she starts to protest.

"You act like you weren't trying to get my attention, but we both know differently. Now get over here."

She slowly makes her way over to me and rests her hands on my knees. I spread my legs for her, giving her plenty of room to stand between them. Slowly, her hands slowly travel up to the tops of my swim trunks before pulling them down just far enough for my dick to pop out.

She eyes it hungrily and wastes no time wrapping her soft hand around it and I swear I could cum just from that touch alone. Even though I'm probably not going to last long, I'm sure as hell planning to try.

"Put your mouth on it. We don't have much time before he gets back." I grit out.

When she does what I ask and steps forward, wrapping her mouth around me, I throw my head back and let out a groan of agony mixed with relief. It feels so damn good to have her hot, wet mouth around me. All I want to do is hammer into her and cum down her throat, but I can't do that to a virgin. We have to work up to that.

Showing her the pace I want, I wrap my hands in her wet hair. Nice and slow is perfect, so I can enjoy her mouth as long as possible.

"Watching you out here with him, swimming, flirting, and making out. I had never been more jealous of my son. Getting to buy this, my hands and lips on your gorgeous body, was worth everything." I mean every word of it.

Aspen would go home and over dinner, I was mad at Brett, though I couldn't verbalize why. I understand it now, but damn if I didn't hate him then.

"When he got that call to pick up his friend, the situation was just too perfect to pass up," I tell her. Her wide eyes look up at me, understanding what day I'm thinking of.

They were in the pool, and I got in before Brett got a call from a friend asking for a ride. Of course, Brett went to help out, leaving Aspen alone for a good forty-five minutes. It was the first time we got some one-on-one time together. While she swam in the pool, I grilled dinner on the porch, and then we talked, even if I wanted to do so much more.

She picks up the pace again and takes even more of me. When she starts gagging around my cock, I know there is no hope of me holding out much longer. I have to let go.

"Fuck, here it comes. Be a good girl and take every drop." I moan just before my seed starts shooting down her throat.

After swallowing every drop, she pulls off me, and looks at me with that sweet innocent face I can't get enough of and want even more.

"Fuck baby, that was so good." Her whole face lights up with the praise and I smile myself.

"Let's go inside and shower, then I will make you dinner," I tell her, offering my hand to help her from the pool.

Before heading inside, I wrap a towel around her. Then I lead her to my bathroom and let the shower warm-up. She looks a little nervous and I realize this will be the first time we see each other fully naked, and I get hard all over again.

"Clothes off and get in the water, baby girl."

She drops the towel and unties her swimsuit, letting it fall to the ground on top of the towel. I don't get time to look at her before she is in the shower, so I remove my swim trunks and follow her.

When I walk in, her head is tilted up, letting the warm water wash over her body and I swear she looks like an angel sent from heaven just for me.

I pick up the soap and start washing her shoulders and working my way down. She watches my every move and despite the warm water, goosebumps race across her skin.

When I lean in for a kiss, it's like she is so desperate to be close to me that she wraps her arms around my neck and presses her body against mine. My cock is hard, and her breasts are pressed against my chest, which isn't helping matters.

Wrapping my arms around her waist, I hold her close, not wanting her to move.

"Do you want me?" I whisper into her ear because I need to be sure she isn't doing this just because of the money. Something inside me needs to know she really wants me.

"Yes. I have wanted you for a long time. Longer than I should have."

Fuck, if I had known that, I don't think I'd have lasted this long before having her.

"Dinner first." I pull away and shut off the water.

# Chapter 11

## Aspen

After dinner, he tells me to go sit on the couch and pick out a movie while he cleans up the kitchen. I try to help but he won't have it, so I do as I'm told and sit on the couch and flip through what movies are available on the steaming channels he has.

I find one about a girl who was dating a spy and haven't seen it yet. It's part comedy and part action and should be something Evan will like too. I can't count how many James Bond movies I've sat through with him and Brett.

He joins me in the living room but doesn't sit close to me. When I look at him about to ask why, he winks at me, and I can tell from his expression this is something else he wants to play out like at the pool.

Just thinking about the pool gets me so wet that I have to shift my thighs a bit for some relief, something that doesn't go unnoticed by him. As the movie starts, he pulls the blanket off the back of the couch and hands it to me.

He knows I love to cuddle under a blanket and watch TV. After the first few times I watched movies at Evan's house, and asked for a blanket, suddenly there was always one on the back of the couch for me to use. To know how considerate he is of me and how aware of me he is, well, it's still as much of a turn-on as if he had his hands on me. He kept something in his house just for me and part of me hopes he thought of me when he looked at it every day.

As I get into the movie, Evan scoots over and uses part of the blanket. Something he has done a few times before, so I don't think anything of it until his hand lands on my thigh. I'm wearing short shorts, so his hand is on my bare skin. That's something new. He's not done that before while we watched TV.

I glance at him, and he gives me a subtle shake of his head and then looks over at the recliner where Brett would normally sit and watch TV. When his dad was watching TV with us, Brett never sat on the couch with me, saying it was too weird.

"Watch TV. Don't want him to know what I'm doing to his girlfriend." He whispers in my ear before turning back to watch the movie and raising his hand higher up my leg.

He spends the rest of the movie touching me everywhere but where I need it. By the end of the movie, I'm tempted to lock myself in the bathroom and finish the job.

"You have no idea how many movies night I sat here with my cock hard and wanting to touch you like that."

"If you don't touch me soon, I'm going to have to do it myself." I moan and squeeze my legs together. He smiles at me, but he has a look in his eyes. If I didn't know any better, I'd say it was close to love.

"What do you need, baby girl?" he asks, scooting even closer to me.

That's easy.

"You."

"I don't think I can be gentle," he says. "I'm too worked up and have wanted you for so long. Once I'm inside you, I'm afraid I'm going to lose my mind." His vulnerability is written all over his face.

"Good. I don't want gentle. I just want you." Then I pull his face down to mine, kissing him to show him I mean what I say.

When he breaks the kiss and stands, the tent in his pants painfully obvious. He takes my hand and leads me upstairs to his room. Waiting for him to tell me what to do, I stand in front of his bed. I love it when he takes charge, and I'm starting to crave it even more.

"Take off your clothes and sit on the edge of the bed." He says, stripping off his shirt.

I don't move. I can't because the sight in front of me has me frozen in place. Even though I just saw him on full display in the shower earlier, it seems so long ago when he is standing in front of me now.

"Don't make me repeat myself," he growls. His tone has me jumping into action. I remove my clothes and do as he asks.

He runs his eyes all over my body and he doesn't even try to hide the heat in them. It gives me the courage to spread my legs even more for him. Then he does the unexpected. He drops to his knees in front of me.

Before I can ask what he is doing, he leans in and latches on to my clit. I'm right back to feeling like I was on the couch earlier. I'm teetering right on the edge of a powerful orgasm. Thankfully, he knows it too and doesn't play too long, bringing his hand up and thrusting two fingers into me.

The fullness of his finger in me sets off my climax as I clench around him. Falling back on the bed, unable to stay upright, he doesn't let up, drawing my pleasure out. When I relax, he nips the inside of my thigh before standing and removing his pants and boxers.

He stands in front of me on full display and despite the earth shattering orgasm which left my bones like jello, I sit up to take his magnificence in. Once again he takes my hand, and this time he turns me around to face the bed, with my back to him. Then he pushes my top half down onto the bed.

"Every time I dream of having you, it's always like this. It's as if I'm sneaking in and doing something I shouldn't be." He kisses my neck and a moment later, his hard cock is at my entrance.

I take a deep breath. This is it. This is the moment for which I've been waiting. Even though I don't know what to expect, my body wants him more than I want my next breath. When he starts to slide into me, I feel so full all I can do I is groan and grip the sheets as he moves with shallow soft thrusts.

As I was waiting for the pain everyone talks about to happen, there doesn't seem to be any until the grip on my hips tightens.

"Fuck. I'm sorry, baby. I tried to go slow, you just feel so damn good, so tight around daddy he can't stop."

Without time for me to think about him using the daddy word, he pushes forward in a hard thrust and the pain I was expecting rips through my body as I scream into the sheets and my legs give out.

He holds me up and bends over my body, kissing my neck and shoulders whispering words about what a good girl I am and how good I feel. After a minute he moves slowly, and the pain is gone replaced by the beautiful stretch of me taking all of him.

His thrusts increase and he grips my shoulders and pulls me up so my back is against his chest, and we can watch ourselves in the mirror on top of his dresser. Watch his cock slide in and out of me and seeing the look of pure ecstasy on his face, it's the hottest thing I've ever seen in my life.

When he reaches up to pinch my nipples, the feeling mixed with the sight in the mirror is too much and I start cumming so hard my legs give out again. He's right there to catch me.

"Fuck, you are even tighter when you cum on my cock." He groans, then speeds his thrusts and his hot seed fills me.

When the last of his cum has been milked from him, he pulls me up onto the bed and wraps his arms around me. We are a sweating mess, and it registers that he didn't use a condom. But I remind myself that the club required me to get on the birth control shot to be in the auction.

For a brief moment, I wish that wasn't the case. I wonder if that's what he wants too, as he rubs my lower belly right where his seed was just planted.

# Chapter 12

## Evan

Fuck, Aspen is so beautiful when she sleeps. Today is the last day of our week together. I have this unbearable need to be inside her to remind her how well I know her body and that she can't leave me.

We haven't talked about what will happen at the end of our week together. She could choose to leave me and that would kill me, even though I'd let her go.

This last week has been perfect. I paid off all her bills, and I loved every minute of doing so because it meant I was taking care of my baby girl. She's done nothing but relax by the pool, on the couch, and in my bed.

She made many comments about not knowing when she last had this much free time. We cuddled on the couch, each reading a book every afternoon after lunch, and then we'd talk about the books over dinner. This isn't a routine I'm ready to give up just yet.

My plan today is to give her orgasm after orgasm until she is physically unable to leave me. Then I will tell her all the reasons why she should stay. That starts with her waking up the same way I plan to wake her up for the rest of my life, with a mind-shattering orgasm.

So, I scoot down the bed and take the blanket with me, exposing her naked body as I go. I've spent the last few days kissing and touching every inch of this soft, silken skin as I go. I have every mark, scar, and blemish memorized and it's all beautiful to me.

Gently rolling her onto her back, I spread her legs. There are little love bites on the inside of her thighs from all the time I've spent down here this week, and I love the evidence of me being here.

I lightly run my tongue over her clit. I'm not ready for her to wake up just yet, but I love how her body reacts even when she is asleep. As she starts to move and come awake, I double down my efforts to bring her to an orgasm while waking up.

I circle her clit with my tongue, and her hand grips my hair.

Backing up a bit, I smile, "Good morning, baby girl." I then go right back to my job, making her cum.

She gasps but otherwise remains quiet as her orgasm builds until she shatters locking her thighs around my head and her hands in my hair. What can I say except it's absolutely blissful.

Now I'm hard as a rock. So I kiss up her body and climb on top of her. As I slide into her, she looks up at me with a huge smile on her face. She is wet and as tight as the first night. Even now it's still like she is strangling my cock. Every time I have to fight not to come the moment I slide into her.

When she takes all of me, I have to pause and bury my head in her neck to gain my composure because this isn't about me. This is proving to her that she needs to stay.

Starting at a slow pace, I finally look into her eyes and all I see is love there. I hope I'm reading her right, not just seeing what I want to see.

"I need more time with you. What will it take?" I ask as I move slowly. If she is trying to move me faster, it won't work. I won't budge until she answers me.

Anything to she could ask for, I would provide. If it's a mansion in Paris, I'd get on the phone right now and buy her one. When she doesn't answer me, I stop.

"I will pay anything," I tell her and she shakes her head.

"All you need to do is ask."

She gasps and tries to move her hips. But I've been waiting for this moment and I have to take my shot.

"Be mine," I say. "I want to take you on dates, show you off, call you mine, and sleep with you in my arms every night. This isn't just some weeklong fling for me."

"That's what I want because this isn't just a fling for me, either. I don't want to walk away today," Aspen says.

"Then don't."

She nods her head and pulls me down for a kiss as I start moving inside of her again. Knowing that she's mine, I swear makes this feel that much better. Neither of us is going to last much longer, but there is one more thing to settle.

"I take care of what is mine, baby girl. Quit your job at the diner and get on doing something you like."

"Okay," she whispers.

I swear there are tears in her eyes, but the smile on her face tells me if there are, they are good tears.

Now that she's finally mine, I need to show her it's not just words. When I say I will take care of her, I need to show her I mean I will in all ways. Starting now.

Angling my hips so I'm hitting just the right spot, I kiss her. With this kiss, I try to tell her how much she means to me and how happy I am she wants to be mine.

A moment later, she is digging her nails into my back and has her legs locked around my waist while screaming my name. With a huge smile on my face, I follow her over the edge and cum harder than I think I ever have. Something about her being mine made this time so much more intense.

Then I roll off her, holding her in my arms while we catch our breath. With her snuggling up to me, it brings me a sense of peace I haven't felt in longer than I can remember.

"You are good at organizing and seem to love it. My office needs it badly. I will pay you to come in and get it back to a manageable state," I offer.

It's true she loves to organize, and my office needs it. What I don't say is that I have to get back to work, but I don't want to leave her. If she comes into the office with me, then it's a win-win.

"Well, I have always wanted to see your office..." she jokes and offers me a big smile.

That smile there, I'm a goner. If I wasn't before, I am now. This girl owns every part of me.

# Chapter 13

## Aspen

E van wasn't joking about his office needing some organization. He told me he's between secretaries since the last one went and got married and put in her notice.

Today is my third day here. The first day, I sorted out the secretary's desk papers, along with all sorts of things, including files that had been laid there and had piled up. Yesterday, I spent the day putting his files away and organizing his filing cabinets. Enjoying that task very much, since I had a direct view of Evan from the filing cabinets in his office.

While filling in as his secretary, I answer the phone and help with his schedule. He had been using his CFO's secretary, so she's been doing double jobs and was very grateful for a break.

Though I think lunchtime is my favorite. Every day, we have lunch together. He doesn't schedule meetings, he transfers the phone to the answering service, and we close the door and spend some time together. Of course, he makes sure I eat, always taking care of me. To say we've been christening every inch of his office would be an understatement.

Right now, I'm sitting at the secretary's desk going over some of his appointments, which are mostly conference phone calls. Because he doesn't like me sitting out here at the desk where he can't see me, Evan had the desk moved so that when his door is open, he can see me. The last time I checked he was on a phone call, so I've just been patiently waiting for lunch.

Getting lost in reading an article online, I nearly jump out of my seat when the pager at the desk goes off.

"Aspen, our lunch is down at the front desk. Will you please go pick it up and bring it here?"

When I jump up and look at him, he's got a small smirk on his face. Nodding, I smooth down my skirt before heading downstairs to get our lunch. Butterflies fill my belly the whole way there and back, knowing what's waiting for me after lunch.

Not for the first time, I wonder if anyone in his office suspects what we do on our lunch break. But even if they do, I know they won't say anything. Although with some of the looks I get, it makes me wonder. They respect him Maybe even fear him. No one dares to bother him if the door is closed. It's an unspoken rule around the office I've come to find out. The fact that his door has been open so much since I've been here hasn't gone unnoticed either.

Once back at his office, I go in and close the door behind me. Standing up from behind his desk, he takes the food from me and sets it up on the coffee table in front of the couch in his office. In just over the week that we've been together, he's already proven how much he paid attention when I wasn't even his. For instance, he can order food for me from just about anywhere and get it right.

Today he ordered from a little farm-to-table restaurant. Both of us got a burger and fries. As usual, the food was delicious, and I enjoyed every bite. During our lunch, Evan talked about one of the new clients that he just brought on. Even if I don't quite understand everything he's talking about, I like that he discusses his work and keeps me in the loop. I recognize the names from his schedule and the calls that I set-up for him, so it's nice to put two and two together.

Almost as soon as we finish our lunch, I can see the shift in him, and I know what time it is. It's time for me to play the role of the secretary. As I stand up and collect all of our stuff from lunch, he clears his throat and stands up over by his desk and picks up a file and starts slipping through it.

"Before you leave, I dropped my pen under the couch. Will you retrieve it for me?" He uses his office voice. While it's a very dismissive tone, I have to say it makes my heart flutter.

To do as he asks, I have to pull the coffee table out just a little and then get down on my knees. Looking under the couch, sure enough, there's a pen at the very back against the wall. At least he gets points for authenticity.

I start reaching for the pen, but at the same time the farther I reach, the higher my butt goes into the air. There's some shuffling behind me as I attempt to reach for the pen. But I wait to see what he has planned next.

"Did you really come to work without any underwear on?" His voice is gruff and much nearer than it was before.

He knows I didn't have underwear on because he was the one who dressed me this morning. But I need to stay in character.

"Yes... I was in a hurry and didn't think it would be a big deal."

"You didn't think it was going to be a big deal flashing that pussy around the office?" His voice is even closer now.

I start to sit up and pull my skirt down.

"You better get that pen for me."

So, I reached back down, stretching for the pen again and there's more shuffling as I move under the couch, trying to get the pen that is just out of my reach.

The shuffling stops and before I can register what is happening, he thrusts himself fully inside of me.

"This is what happens when little girls tease men." He says, reaching over me, grabbing my breasts over my shirt and squeezing hard.

I try to stop myself from crying out because it all feels so good. This is what I've been waiting for all morning. I guess I wasn't as quiet as I needed to be because just as I'm about to orgasm the door opens.

When I look up, there is my ex, Brett, with some new girl. My body instantly heats in embarrassment. Though I am still expecting Evan to jump up and try to explain, he doesn't even pull out of me. Instead, he places a hand on my lower back keeping me in place, and yells at Brett to get out.

Brett's eyes are glued to me, and a visible shudder runs through him. Even from here, I can the disgusted look on his face.

"I said get out!" Evan yells again, and that seems to snap Brett out of it.

"Yeah, we will talk about this at home," Brett says before taking the girl's hand, turning around, and slamming the door behind him.

Evan leans over me and places his mouth by my ear.

"You will cum, baby girl," He growls. Then he starts moving in me. His thrusts are at a savage pace, like he's angry, and I supposed he is at Brett for interrupting us. How can I be this embarrassed at my ex finding us, but still so turned on that I'm on the edge of an orgasm?

When his hand trails over my hip and plays with my clit, it's just enough to ignite an explosion in me. He barely gets his hand on my mouth before I cum hard all over him.

That triggers his release, and he buries his head in my neck to muffle his own groan as he cums inside of me. Then he rests his head on my shoulder and neither of us moves for a moment before he pulls out and helps clean me up.

Once we are all fixed up, he pulls me into his arms.

"I guess it's time to go face the music." He sighs and my heart sinks.

# Chapter 14

## Evan

As soon as I say it's time to go face the music, I can feel her body tense and I can only imagine what's running through her mind.

"This changes nothing between us. I still want you as much as I did before."

She nods her head that's against my chest, but it's halfhearted.

"I'll let you talk," she says, pulling away. But I only grip her tighter.

"Oh, no baby girl, you are going in there by my side."

Then I gather our things and head out before she can come up with another excuse. The drive home is quiet and I'm sure a lot is running through her head. I hold her hand, letting her know I'm here and I want her.

Even though I hate how sad she looks, and I want nothing more than to try to cheer her up, but now isn't the time. Words are one thing, but what happens once we get to my house will be another.

When we walk into the house, Brett is there sitting on the couch and the girl he was with earlier is sitting next to him, and she looks extremely uncomfortable. Well, I can't really blame her. This is not going to be the best way to meet the boyfriend's dad for the first time.

Brett looks up when he hears me, but then gives the most disgusted look to Aspen. For the first time in my life, I really want to punch my son with all my strength. She's mine now, and that means it's my job to protect her. Though he may be my son, I raised him better than how he treated her, so we're going to have a lot to talk about.

"Why is she here?" Brett nods in revulsion toward Aspen and even though I'm just holding her hand, I can feel the tension rise in her.

"Because she's been invited here. Who's this?" I direct my attention toward the girl whose name I still don't know sitting next to my son.

"This is Elana, my fiancé. I was bringing her home for you to meet her." He sounds cocky, like he thinks he has the upper hand, but he's about to find out that I never go into anything without a plan.

That name sounds vaguely familiar, and I try to put the pieces together.

"This is the girl you dumped Aspen for."

"Yeah, well, I didn't expect to find you fucking my ex-girlfriend. What the fuck were you thinking?"

"You will watch how you talk to me in my house."

We stand there for a minute staring each other down, but he finally gives me a quick nod, so I continue.

"I could say the same thing about you dumping Aspen just because her mom got sick, and she wouldn't put out. I'm disgusted with you."

His face goes pale, knowing he's being called out. There's no real argument to give the girl he's with whose name I've already forgotten who gives him a disgusted look. Thankfully, she keeps silent. At least she knows her place.

"The feeling is mutual then," he says as he crosses his arms and glares at me. The girl sitting next to him looks like she wants to die and crawl into a hole just to get out of this situation.

As I'm about to reply, Aspen yanks her hand out of mine and runs upstairs. I don't even think. I turn and follow her. Before she goes into the bedroom, I catch up with her, and wrap my arms around her waist. Then I pull her into the room and close the door behind us before pressing her up against the door.

"No, I... no, let me go home," her voice shaky. Even though Aspen's trying to keep her composure and be strong, she doesn't have to be.

"I told you this changes nothing between us and I meant what I said. I'm not letting you go." When I tighten my grip on her, she shakes her head and places a hand on my chest, pushing me back. Even that slight distance between us makes me hate every bit of it.

"Please. Let me go home. You stay here and talk to him. Later tonight when you're done, you can come over to my house. This is horrible because I never wanted to get in between you two. I know how important he is to you, and I have a lot to process as well."

I know she means finding out that Brett's getting married. That news must have been a shock and I should be there for her. It's what I want to be. Someone that she can lean on, talk to and vent about all this.

Though I'm conflicted about what she actually needs. While I know she's telling me to go talk to Brett and that she needs time to process, I don't know if that's what she actually needs or if she should even be left alone right now.

In the end, I have to trust her because it goes both ways. If I want her to trust me, then I have to trust her as well. So, I lean in and kiss her gently at first but deeper, needing to let her know exactly how I feel in this kiss. Though there's something about this kiss which seems really important to me even though I can't put my finger on it.

She wraps her arms around my neck and kisses me back before she pulls away and offers me a wobbly smile. As she gathers her things, I stand there not wanting to miss out on a moment with her and then walk her to the door, kissing her again before she leaves. Taking a deep breath, I turn and go back to the family room at the back of the house where Brett is waiting.

When I walk into the room, they both have their noses on their phones, and I can only imagine who they're talking to right now.

"We need to talk," I say. Then I glare at my son.

# Chapter 15

## Aspen

I don't even remember getting home, just collapsing on the couch and crying. No matter how much Evan stressed that it doesn't change things between us, in a way it does. That's his son, his family, his flesh and blood. As much as I hate to admit it, Brett should be important as me.

But then I also didn't want him to see me fall apart. Something about finding out Brett had proposed to this girl, and that she was the one that he dumped me for just hit harder than I expected. While I knew he would be dating, I didn't really care. But I just never thought I'd have to come face to face with her.

It's not that I still have feelings for Brett because I don't. At least not like that. Yet because of everything that was going on with my mom, I don't think I ever fully healed from what he did to me. Instead, I tucked it away and moved on because my mom needed me. Though I never dealt with it all, but now I don't have a choice.

Pulling myself up off the couch, I go into the kitchen and grab a tub of ice cream and a spoon. I also get my tablet and collapse back on the couch. Trying to distract myself with pointless videos online, I decide to look at my email first and check if I have anything from Willow. Seeing her message with the phone number and instructions to call her, I glance at the time. Since she's in Montana, which is an hour behind me, it's not too late. So I get my phone and give her a call.

"Hello." a deep gruff voice answers the phone.

"Can I speak to Willow, please?" I ask. Though he doesn't say anything right away and I almost wonder if we've been disconnected.

"Who is this?" he sounds almost pissed off.

"Oh, my name is Aspen. Willow and I..."

"Hang on." He interrupts me without a second thought. Then there are some muffled voices before Willow finally takes the phone.

"Aspen? Are you safe? Did you make money? What happened?"

"Calm down there, tiger. I'm fine. I'm safe. I made more money than I thought possible, but I need to know that you're safe too and that you're okay."

"I'm plenty safe. Bennett won't let anything happen to me. By the way, that was my husband, Bennett, who answered the phone."

"So, you went through with it? You did marry him?"

"Yeah, but it is completely not what I was expecting. He lives up here on the mountain in a kind of secluded area. But his friends are really nice and all of them are married. It's nice that their wives accepted me without a second thought. And I actually love it out here in Montana. It's so peaceful and relaxing. But the best of all is that with Bennett it was love at first sight." I can hear the goofy smile on her face, and I know that smile. It's been a long time since she's had that smile on her face and I'm really happy for her.

"Now tell me what happened at the auction. Did I understand your email right? Brett's dad bought you?"

The next half hour is spent going over all the details of the auction and leading up to what happened tonight. All while stuffing my mouth full of ice cream.

"Wow, I don't even know what to say," she remarks after I finish telling her everything.

"That about sums it up. So here I am eating ice cream tonight instead of spending the night with him like planned."

"I know this is going to sound like a stupid question, but are you all right?" she asks.

Even so far away, I can hear the genuine concern in her voice. That's one thing I like about Willow, you can always tell that she genuinely cares.

"Yes... No... I don't know. I knew it couldn't last, but I just didn't think it would go like this. Even though I had it all built up in my head that he was going to have a talk with his son, I knew it wouldn't go smoothly, but I expected it to go better than this."

"I bet he comes for you tonight. Just wait and see," Willow says, always the optimist.

"I don't know. But then there's his son and I don't think he'll want to lose that relationship. They haven't always had it easy, but I know that his son means the world to him. Even when I was with Brett, I could tell how close they were."

After talking for a while longer, I could tell she was trying to distract me, which I appreciated.

Before we hang up, Willow tells me I can call her at that number anytime, so I made sure to save it. Then I turned off the TV, put what was left of the ice cream away, and went to bed. With any luck, I can get to sleep and wake up feeling better and have all this be behind me.

I checked my phone before going to bed. There was nothing from Evan and my heart sinks. I was hoping for at least a goodnight text. Something, anything to let me know that he's thinking about me, even with everything going on. I lay in bed tossing and turning and I'm not quite sure when I fall asleep.

Waking up in the middle of the night, I start to panic because I feel arms around me holding me so tight, I can't move. But when I try to move, there's a groan from the person behind me.

"Go back to sleep, baby girl. I got you," Evan says with sleep evident in his voice.

"How did you get in here?"

"Last week when you were at my house, I had a copy of your house key made just in case."

"You did what?" I ask in shock as I turn in his arms to face him.

"I meant what I said Aspen, I'm not letting you go."

My mind races ecstatically that he's here. But at the same time, shocked that he's here. Though there is one thing that I'm able to vocalize.

"But Brett..."

# Chapter 16

## Evan

"Brett has to explain to his fiancée why he is still so hung up on you. That's an awkward conversation that they're going to have to get through. What upset him the most was that I told him he was going to have to get used to calling you Mom. "With those words, a smile creeps across her face and she looks up at me.

There's enough light between the streetlight outside and the night light that she keeps in her room that I can see her eyes are wide open and the shock on her face.

"Do you know why I haven't used a condom once?" I chuckle as her face does that little squished-up book she gets when she's concentrating or thinking about something.

"Because the auction made me get on birth control?" she says, answering my question. Pure anger surges through me. I guess that's what I get for not paying attention to the event that we were attending because I had no intention of leaving with anyone. Had I known Aspen was going to be there, I would have read every detail.

"The fuck?"

"Yeah, the club made sure that we were all on the shot before we could even sign up for the auction."

"No more of that shit. I want you pregnant and I don't want anything stopping me. Or stopping us because I want a family with you. And yes, I want to marry you. We can live here in your house, we can live at my house, or we can sell both and get our own place together. Whatever you want to do, I don't care. All I want is you as my wife. Everything else is just details."

Then I pull a ring out of my pocket. It's the one that I bought last week when I made the decision that I was going to keep her. When I slide the ring on her finger, she just sits there staring at it and I have to admit it looks damn good on her hand.

"I meant what I said, and I know you have your doubts, but I have no doubts in my mind. I want to marry you and want to spend the rest of my life loving you and taking care of you. Will you marry me?"

She gasps in shock, and I hope it's a good sign. Finally, she manages to take her eyes off the ring and looks up at me once again with tears in her eyes. Then she handcuffs the back of my neck, pulls me down so her lips are on mine, which sends all my senses into overdrive.

"Yes!" This time when her lips meet mine it says, my fiancé, my forever. And I think it's time we mark this occasion.

I roll her onto her side so that her back is up against my chest and pull her back to me. Quickly, I pull my boxers and pants down and slide into her. She felt incredible before but there are just no words that compare now that I'm sliding into my fiancé.

It just feels different. More intense. I want to draw this out and make love to her all night. But I know my girl. I know she was stressing about this about us all night, which means she really needs her rest. But I really wanted to hold her and reassure her I'm not going anywhere.

I take my job of taking care of her seriously, and she will learn that quickly. So instead of going slow and dragging it out, my thrusts are fast and hurried. My hand sneaks down to her clit to play with her, but she was already so wet that it doesn't take long before I feel the telltale flutter of her walls on my cock.

The closer she gets, the louder she becomes, and I'm right there with her. It feels pretty damn good, and we have no reason to be quiet tonight. When she falls over the edge screaming my name, I swear I've never heard a more beautiful sound.

She is choking my cock, so tight, wet and perfect. Best of all, she's mine. Light reflects on her ring, and it hits me again that after all this time this girl is mine. That thought alone is enough to send me into a powerful orgasm cumming with her name on my lips, holding on to her for dear life.

All night, I hold her close until she drifts off. As much as I love holding her at night, I love waking up with her in my arms even more. After making sure my girl is well taken care of, I finally allow her out of bed and make her breakfast while she gets ready and packs a bag to come stay at my place until we decide where exactly we want to settle down. I told her I don't want her to make a decision now, but to think about it. We can alternate between her place and mine, and that idea seemed to make her happy.

When we pull into my place, Brett's car is still there, and she looks over at me. I could see the question in her eyes before she even opens her mouth.

"They stayed the night here, which is why I came to you."

Even though she nods, I can tell she's uncomfortable and as far as I'm concerned, this house is as much hers as it is mine and I won't have her uncomfortable in her own home.

When we walk in, Brett and his fiancé are sitting at the dining room table eating breakfast. Honestly, I'm shocked they're up this early at all, but now it's as good a time as any.

"I made good on my promise, Brett. Aspen here has agreed to marry me." I steer Aspen into the room, and there's a huge smile on my face that I couldn't stop if I tried.

"Are you kidding me? Elana and I worked things out, but she still isn't okay with having my ex in the picture."

His fiancé has enough sense to look at least a little sorry. But I shake my head because nothing is going to change my mind.

"Too bad, because she's going to be my wife. And I trust her around you because I will keep her happy and satisfied so she won't want anyone but me. Isn't that right, baby girl?" I ask. There's a hint of a smile on her face.

"Yes," she says a bit shyly. We're standing in our house and hiding is not an option here.

"Yes, who?" I say waiting for her to give me the answer I want. She's hesitant, but then a big smile crosses her face.

"Yes, daddy."

"That's fucked up," Brett says, shaking his head as he gets up and walks away. The fiancé eyes us for a moment, but then turns and follows Brett. I just smile. He can say anything he wants because in the end I got the girl, and she wants me just as much as I want her.

# Epilogue

## Aspen

### One month later

**M**oney sure can get you anything you want, including a fall wedding planned in a month. Even at a top wedding venue. Once Evan proposed, he was insistent on getting married as soon as possible.

It wasn't even three days after we told Brett and his fiancé that we were getting married that his fiancé ended things and left. Apparently, she was not okay with me being in the picture permanently. She thought with Brett upset about his dad dating me that we would break up and I'd be out of the picture. When that didn't happen, she left.

Here we are about a month later and Brett could care less. He told his dad that he's realized he never really loved her. What he loved was the idea of her.

Slowly, Brett and his dad have been working things out. About one a month, Brett comes into town, and they have dinner together. Also, they talk a few nights a week on the phone. Brett finally asked the hard questions like what really happened with his mother. It was hard for him to find out that his mother wasn't the love of his father's life, but he admitted in his heart he kind of knew that already.

One night when we were lying in bed talking, I jokingly told Evan that maybe we should wait to have sex again until our wedding night. An idea which he was not happy with, though he said if that's what I wanted he'd do it. I said it wasn't what I wanted, but I felt like we should have something special for our wedding night. Something new.

Now I'm wishing I had just kept my mouth shut because he has me walking down the aisle with a butt plug. Tonight he has plans on taking that virginity from me so that I will be completely his.

While walking down the aisle with a butt plug wasn't exactly what I had in mind, I am excited for tonight. All month, he's been making sure that I'm well prepared.

Willow and her husband flew in for the wedding. Not only is Willow my maid of honor, but she's also walking me down the aisle because she's the closest thing I have to family. Brett finally agreed to be Evan's best man, though he's not hidden the times he finds us cringe worthy.

Moments like us kissing at the rehearsal last night, or that his dad had a bachelor party even if it was just having drinks at the local bar seemed to embarrass him.

"Would you stop shifting? I'm trying to finish buttoning you into this dress!" Willow says from behind me.

Not even she knows the reason that I can't sit still. Every time I move, I feel the butt plug, and then I try to shift to get it back to where it was because it moves every time. It's going to be so hard to stand still in front of everyone while we say our vows. But I know my soon-to-be husband will have a huge smile on his face the entire time.

I mumble a sorry as she finishes getting me buttoned up so we can head out and get some photos before the wedding. Evan went all out and got some big-name photographer to do all of our wedding photos. He was insistent because he didn't want to forget a moment of today.

Photos go by in a blur, and before I know it, the time is upon us. Willow is ready to walk me down the aisle. The music starts playing and the doors open and before I even take that first step, my eyes find Evan. Then we lock in on each other. Being able to watch his eyes run over me and even so far back, I can tell he has tears in his eyes. He's shifting his weight from foot to foot and has to look down for a moment before he looks back up, the tears in his eyes clearly visible now.

We walk past willow's husband who has been scaring people since they got here the other night. He's a big burly mountain man who doesn't seem to care whether people like him. All he cares about is Willow, her safety and her needs. It's all I could ever hope for her. Even now he's sitting as close to the front as he could get and there are eighty seats on either side of him and behind him.

Bennett, Willow's husband, was none too happy about being locked out of the bridal suite, but I needed girl time. Now that he's got eyes on her again, you can see him visibly relax. Mostly he reminds me a lot of Evan and I think the two of them will get along great.

The moment that I'm standing in front of him, he quickly pulls me into his arms, which earn a few chuckles from our friends and family. When my eyes are locked with Evans, it's as if I'm pulled into a trance. Even though the ceremony goes on around us, and they say all the right words at the right time, but it's just the two of us in this moment.

Then his lips are on mine. It's official. This man is now my husband. A moment I dreamed about but never thought would happen. Wasting no time, he gets me back down the aisle and back into the room where I got ready. He made it very clear in the wedding planning that everyone is to go and have some cocktails before we do any photos because he didn't want to wait to have me for the first time as his wife. He insisted everything I wear be easy access and it is including the fact that I have no underwear on. The moment that his hand reaches up, and he realizes I'm bare, it's like all controls snap.

"Did you really walk down the aisle to me with your pussy bare?" I bite my lip and nod my head, waiting to see what he does next.

"Thank fuck. It's a good thing I didn't know that or I would have bent you over and had my dick inside you while we were saying our vows. Right there in front of everyone."

Why the hell does that idea turn me on so damn much? With a hard kiss on my lips, he spins me around and pushes my hands down onto the vanity. My dress is bunched up in the back and I can feel the cool air on my ass. When he plays with the butt plug, slowly turning it, all I can do is moan.

"Feels good, doesn't it, baby girl?" I'm so focused on the sensations from him playing with the butt plug, I don't even feel his cock at my entrance until he's thrusting all the way in. With the butt plug in, he feels that much bigger, and he has to fight his way in because there's no room.

"I think this is the time I put a baby in that belly. I'm willing to bet you I can feel it."

The birth control that I had to get to be in the auction should be wearing off anytime. That's a fact that Evan has not forgotten. He's certain that the first chance he gets, he's going to knock me up. I've always wanted to be a mom and since Evans has been through it all before, it's like having a cheat sheet to raise the baby.

Looking in the mirror of him behind me, I see pure bliss on his face being inside of me. That alone is enough to set me close to the edge, but when his hand reaches around and plays with my clit, I don't have a chance in hell of holding my orgasm back. Turning my head to the side, he captures my mouth with his, just in time as the most intense pleasure races to my body, weakening every muscle. If I wasn't leaning on the vanity, I'm sure I'd have collapsed. When he cums hard and fast, collapsing onto me, I know he's feeling the same way. Things have always been intense with us. But even more so after he asked me to marry him, and I officially became his fiancé and even more so now as his wife.

He pulls out of me and helps me clean up and fix my dress before kissing me again.

"Just remember, my wife, tonight your ass is mine." His words alone have him hard again. As we walk back out to our wedding reception, there's a huge smile on his face.

• • • • ● • ● • • •

Want more Aspen and Evan? **Get a bonus Epilogue now!**

Want Willows story? Read it in **Take Me To The Mountain.**

**Get more Club Red in Elusive Dom.**

# Connect with Kaci Rose

**Website**

**Facebook**

**Kaci Rose Reader's Facebook Group**

**TikTok**

**Instagram**

**Twitter**

**Goodreads**

**Book Bub**

## Join Kaci Rose's VIP List (Newsletter)

# Other Books by Kaci Rose

See all of Kaci Rose's Books

**Oakside Military Heroes Series**
**Saving Noah** – Lexi and Noah
**Saving Easton** – Easton and Paisley
**Saving Teddy** – Teddy and Mia
**Saving Levi** – Levi and Mandy
**Saving Gavin** – Gavin and Lauren
**Saving Logan** – Logan and Faith


**Mountain Men of Whiskey River**
**Take Me To The River** – Axel and Emelie
**Take Me To The Cabin** – Pheonix and Jenna
**Take Me To The Lake** – Cash and Hope

**Taken by The Mountain Man** - Cole and Jana
**Take Me To The Mountain** – Bennett and Willow

**Chasing the Sun Duet**
**Sunrise** – Kade and Lin
**Sunset** – Jasper and Brynn

**Rock Stars of Nashville**
**She's Still The One** – Dallas and Austin

**Club Red – Short Stories**
**Daddy's Dare** – Knox and Summer
**Sold to my Ex's Dad** - Evan and Jana
**Jingling His Bells**

**Club Red: Chicago**
**Elusive Dom**

**Standalone Books**
**Texting Titan** - Denver and Avery
**Accidental Sugar Daddy** – Owen and Ellie
**Saving Mason** - Mason and Paige

**Stay With Me Now** – David and Ivy
**Midnight Rose** - Ruby and Orlando
**Committed Cowboy** – Whiskey Run Cowboys
**Stalking His Obsession** - Dakota and Grant
**Falling in Love on Route 66** - Weston and Rory
**Billionaire's Marigold**
**Saving Ethan**
**Decking the Don**

# About Kaci Rose

Kaci Rose writes steamy contemporary romance mostly set in small towns. She grew up in Florida but longs for the mountains over the beach.
She is a mom to 5 kids and a dog who is scared of his own shadow.

She also writes steamy cowboy romance as Kaci M. Rose.

# Please Leave a Review!

I love to hear from my readers! Please **head over to your favorite store and leave a review** of what you thought of this book!

Made in the USA
Columbia, SC
24 September 2024

42931381R00067